# Call Me Tree
## Llámame árbol

Maya Christina González

translation/traducción Dana Goldberg

Children's Book Press, *an imprint* of Lee & Low Books Inc., New York

I begin
Within
The deep
　　dark
　　　earth

Nazco
Dentro
De la tierra
　profunda
　y oscura

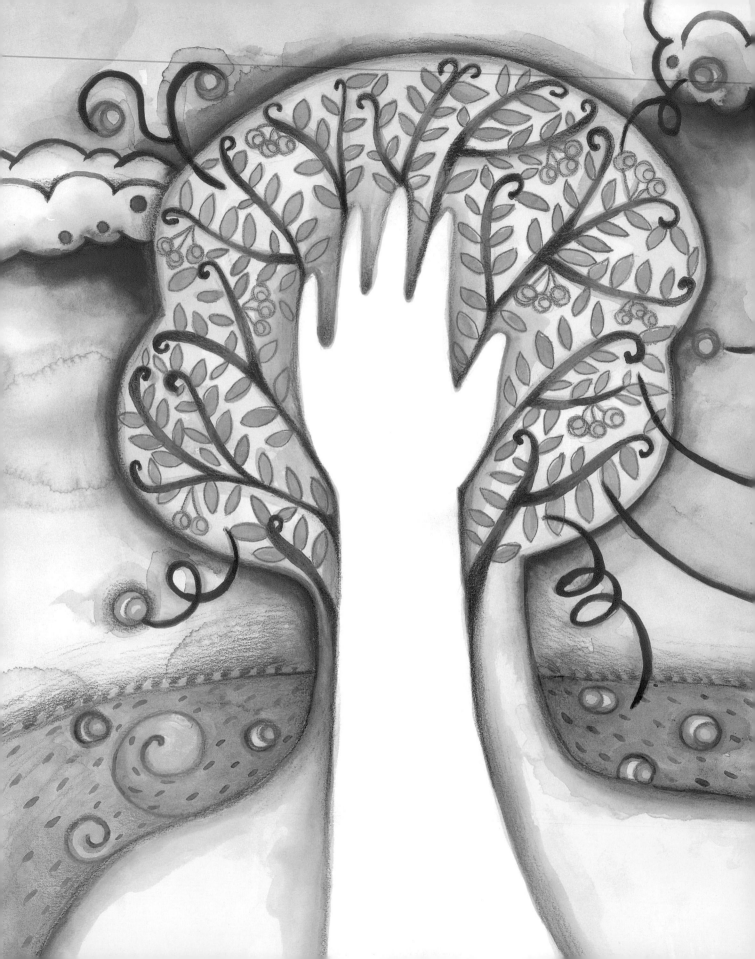

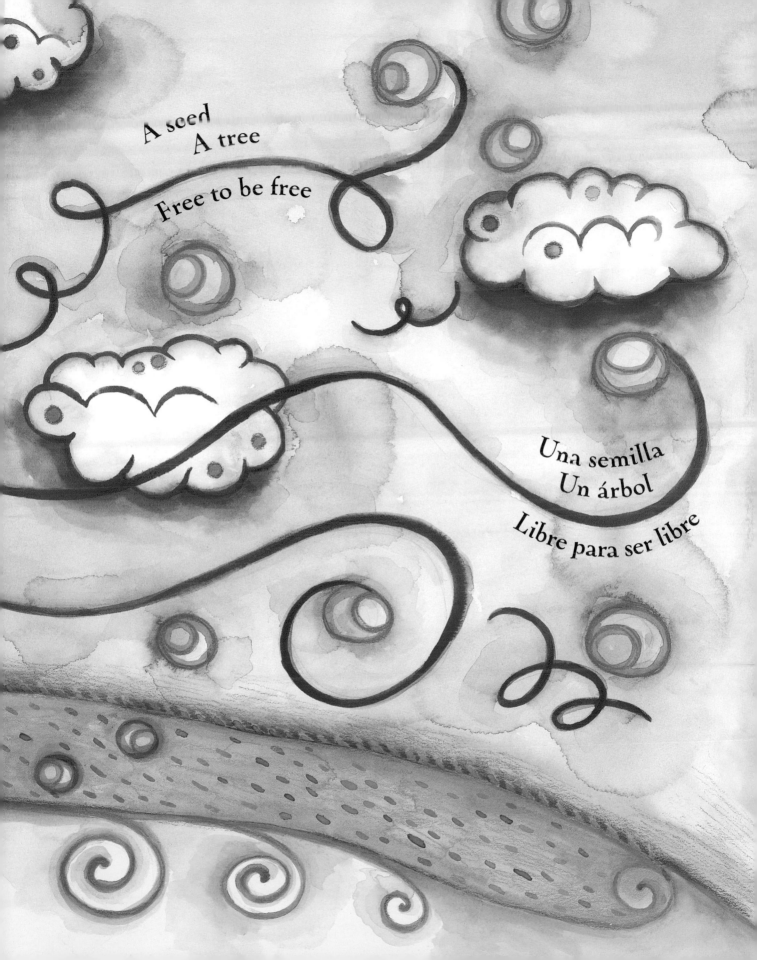

A seed
A tree

Free to be free

Una semilla
Un árbol

Libre para ser libre

I dream
I am reaching
Dreaming and reaching
Reaching and dreaming

Yo sueño
Me extiendo
Sueño y me extiendo
Me extiendo y sueño

I wake UP
I see sky
Sky as high
As a bird
Can fly

Me DESPIERTO
Veo el cielo
El cielo tan alto
Como puede volar
Un pájaro

I reach
And I rise

Me extiendo
Y me elevo

And what do I see
With my eyes
As I rise?

Y ¿qué veo
Con mis ojos
Mientras me elevo?

A tree I am
A tree I stand

Un árbol soy
De pie estoy

On a sidewalk
En la acera

On a mountain
En la montaña

By a river or a road
Junto al río o al camino

Some trees reach
Some trees teach
Some trees stand so still

Algunos árboles se extienden
Algunos árboles enseñan
Algunos árboles se quedan
tan quietos

Some sing songs
Some sing along
All trees have roots
All trees belong

Unos cantan canciones
Otros se unen al coro
Todos los árboles tienen raíces
Todos los árboles tienen un lugar

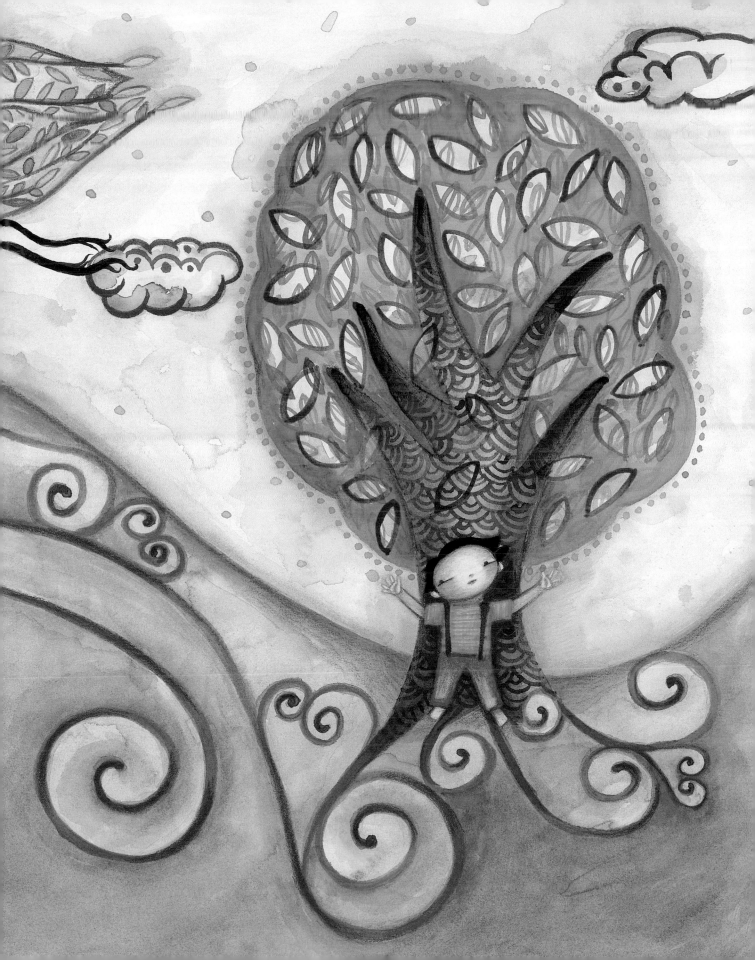

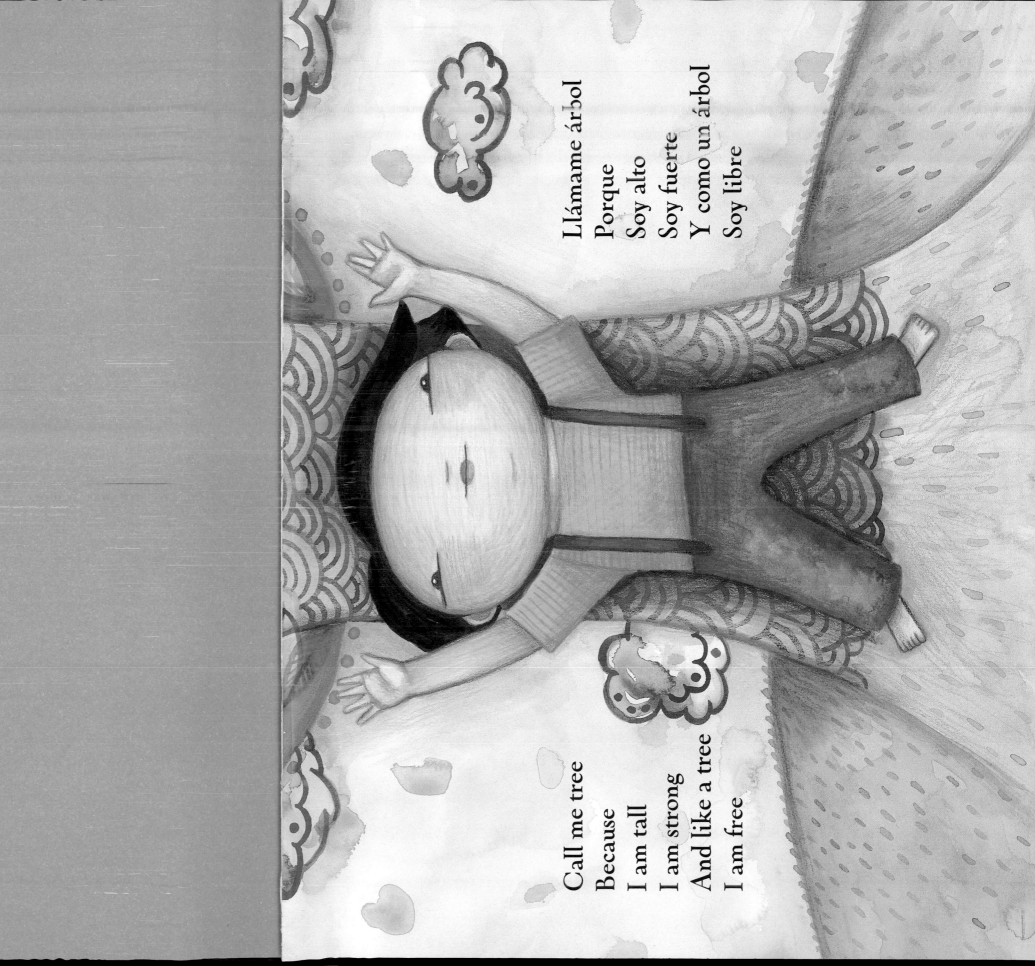

Call me tree
Because
I am tall
I am strong
And like a tree
I am free

Llámame árbol
Porque
Soy alto
Soy fuerte
Y como un árbol
Soy libre

To all the beautiful trees I have met, and especially to my trees: Matthew, Zai, and Sky, XO —M.C.G.

My family moved to the Oregon woods when I was thirteen. After living in the desert, the trees amazed me. I lived in the deep woods again as a young adult. Surrounded by huge, majestic trees, I got to know their unique characteristics and how they changed throughout the year. Each had a presence and spirit. I considered the trees friends and part of my world. And at times I thought of myself as a tree! I still do. Trees teach me so much about being free, being exactly who I am, everyone belonging, and much more. I like to see kids as trees. In the illustrations, I included some kids in the yoga tree pose. I loved doing the tree pose when I was young: balancing, being strong and stable. I'll call you tree if you call me tree!

Love,

Matthew Smith-Gonzalez

**MAYA CHRISTINA GONZALEZ** loves trees, rivers, and colors, among many other things. She has illustrated more than twenty picture books, several of which have won recognition from the Pura Belpré Award, Américas Book Award, and International Latino Book Awards. This is the third book Gonzalez has both written and illustrated. She lives in San Francisco, California, with her two children and her husband.

The illustrations are rendered in watercolors, inks, and colored pencils
Spanish translation by Dana Goldberg
Book design by Carl Angel
Book production by The Kids at Our House
The text is set in Oneleigh Bold
Manufactured in China by Toppan, July 2014
10 9 8 7 6 5 4 3 2 1
First Edition

Library of Congress Cataloging-in-Publication Data

Gonzalez, Maya Christina.

Call me tree / Maya Christina Gonzalez ; translation, Dana Goldberg = Llámame árbol / Maya Christina Gonzalez ; traducción, Dana Goldberg.
First edition.

pages cm

Summary: "A bilingual poetic tale that follows one child/tree from the depths of Mami/Earth to the heights of the sky, telling a story about being free to grow and be who we are meant to be and honoring our relationship with the natural world"— Provided by publisher.

ISBN 978-0-89239-294-0 (hardcover : alk. paper)
[1. Stories in rhyme. 2. Trees—Fiction. 3. Spanish language materials—Bilingual.] I. Goldberg, Dana, translator. II. Title. III. Title: Llámame árbol.
PZ74.3.G6 2014
[E]—dc23
2014008759

MIX
Paper from responsible sources
FSC® C104723